CONTENTS

By David Oakden

Illustrated by Robin Lawrie

First published in 2007
by Anglia Young Books

Anglia Young Books is a division of
Mill Publishing
PO Box 120
Bangor
County Down
BT19 7BX

Illustrations by Robin Lawrie
Design by Adrian Baggett

British Library Cataloguing-in-Publication Data

A catalogue record for this book is available from the British Library

ISBN 1-904936-10-5

Printed in Great Britain by Ashford Colour Press, Gosport, Hampshire

THE PEDLAR

Thomas came into the cottage. He looked
very angry.

'So much for our good King Henry the
Eighth,' he said.

His wife Martha was putting some sticks on
the fire. The smoke rose through a hole in
the thatched roof.

'What's happened?' she asked.

Thomas sat down on a wooden stool and took off his jerkin.

He lifted his filthy shirt and scratched himself.

'I thought our king was going to stop all this,' he said.

'All what?' said Martha.

'The rich taking our land,' said Thomas, spitting on to the earth floor. 'That's what.'

He went on. 'I'm thirty years old, Martha. I'm getting old. Everything is changing. When we first worked for Sir William we could graze our own sheep and cattle anywhere we liked. And our pig could trot up to the woods to feed on nuts and roots.'

Martha nodded. 'And our geese got fat on the village pond,' she said.

Thomas sighed. 'I found a fence round the bottom of Shooter's Hill today. Sir William has taken over that land, too, for his new flock of sheep.'

Martha looked thoughtful. She went to her spinning wheel. Some sheep's wool was hanging on the wooden frame, ready to be spun. 'That's bad for you,' she said. 'But more sheep will mean cheap wool for spinning. I shall be able to spin it and weave it and make more clothes to keep us warm. The fence may not be such a bad thing.'

Thomas was about to argue with Martha when a shadow filled the open doorway. A man stood on the stone step with a pedlar's pack on his shoulder. 'God bless all here,' he said.

'What have you got to sell?' asked Martha. She liked to see things for sale, even though money was short. 'I need a new comb.'

The man put his pack down but did not open it. 'I have combs – and scissors too,' he said. Then he came up to the fire to warm himself. 'My name's Otto and I've just come back from the wars up in the north. I got a bad sword wound in my back.'

'You poor man,' said Martha. 'Sit down and share some food with us. Thomas, fetch him a jug of ale.' Then she called the children from outside. 'Mary, James, get some more wood for the fire.'

Before long, there was a large iron pan of vegetable soup warming on the blazing fire. Rough barley bread was on the table.

Otto looked round the room. He could see two knives, some wooden spoons and bowls, some beakers and a nice jug. And there was a big wooden chest by the door, too. He smiled to himself.

It was time for the family to eat. They all sat down. Martha said a short prayer of thanks and gave out bowls of thick soup and hunks of bread.

The children ate their food and stared at Otto who was eating very fast. 'You were very hungry,' said Mary when he had finished.

Otto smiled. 'Yes, I was, young lady,' he said, but he wasn't looking at Mary. He was looking at the wooden spoons.

'Father made those spoons,' said James. 'He carved them out of wood from the beech trees in the forest.'

'And he made the bowls, too,' said Mary.

'Come on, children,' said Thomas. 'I need help with the cow. She may have her calf today. We shall have to spread dry grass and <u>bracken</u> for her to lie on.'

Mary ran after her father. While Otto wasn't looking, James had a quick peep in the pedlar's pack, then he followed Mary outside.

Otto sat by the fire and pretended to be asleep.

Martha wanted to see what he had to sell but she didn't like to wake him. Then the baby started crying. Quickly she picked him up. 'Come on, my love,' she said. 'I'll take you outside so you don't wake Otto. We'll look in his pack later.'

As soon as he was alone, Otto opened his eyes. He got his pack and threw in the spoons, the bowls, the knives, the jug and the beakers. Then he went to the wooden chest by the door. It had woollen clothes in it, and Otto put as many as he could into his pack. He took everything from the baby's cot, too.

There was a noise outside. Otto picked up his pack, ran out of the door and made for the forest. Martha saw him. 'Wait,' she called. 'I want one of your combs.'

But he was gone into the trees. Martha went back into the house. The baby's wooden cot was near the door, but all the clothes from it had gone. The wooden chest was empty, too, and everything had been taken off the table.

Martha screamed and called for Thomas. He came running and so did James and Mary. Martha was crying. 'That pedlar,' she

sobbed. 'He's stolen all our things. Your winter woollen cloak and all the baby's clothes, our shoes, our knives and all the bowls and spoons. And to think I gave him some of our food.'

Mary said, 'I thought he was a bit strange. He was staring at everything in the room. And when you went to get the soup he asked me what was in the chest.'

'Yes,' said James. 'And his bag was just full of rubbish. I peeped into it and I didn't see any combs or scissors.'

'I'm going to find him,' said Thomas and he ran towards the forest.

But he was soon back. 'There's no sign of him,' he said and he sat down and put his head in his hands.

Mary started to cry. Martha put her arms round her.

Suddenly there was some noisy shouting outside and the sound of a horse neighing. Everyone went to see what was happening.

And there was Otto! His hands were tied behind his back and there was a rope round his body attached to the horse. The man riding the horse was the thief-catcher, the Catchpole.

Otto was shouting, 'I did nothing. I'm a poor wounded soldier just back from the war. Everything in the pack is mine.'

The Catchpole got off his horse and tore open the pedlar's pack. 'Oh yes,' he said. 'You wear baby's clothes, do you? And little girl's shoes? And as for the wooden things, I helped Thomas make them so I know they belong to him.'

The Catchpole pointed at Otto. 'He's wearing your cloak, Thomas,' he said. He pulled the cloak from Otto's shoulders. 'And

look, see that torn corner? Well, he was
trying to climb over the new fence when the
cloak got caught in it. I saw him and
recognized the cloak.'

The pedlar was on his knees. 'No use
praying,' said the Catchpole. 'The <u>magistrate</u>
will probably see you hanged for this.' Then
he bent down and tore off Otto's shirt.

'Look,' said Martha. 'His skin has no mark on

it, but he told us he was wounded by a sword.'

The Catchpole dragged Otto to the fire. He took out his dagger and held it to the flames until the dagger's point was red hot.

'Here's a little reward for upsetting our good people,' he said. He caught hold of Otto's ear with his left hand. There was a sizzling sound as he twisted the dagger and punched a hole in the pedlar's ear.

Otto screamed with pain. The children covered their eyes and Martha turned the baby's face away. There was a smell of burnt flesh.

The Catchpole wet a cloth in cold water and held it to the ear. 'That's a hole that will never heal,' he said. 'So people will always know that you are a thief. That is, if the magistrate spares your life.'

'Sir William is the magistrate,' said Martha.

'He is a just man.'

'Huh!' said Thomas. He was thinking of Sir William's fence.

The Catchpole mounted his horse and set off, dragging Otto behind him. 'Keep his pack,' he called. 'It may be of use, and he won't want it, not where he's going!'

Martha put back the things Otto had stolen. Then she had a surprise. Right at the bottom of the pack was a small wooden doll. Mary saw it. 'That's my doll!' she said. 'I lost it weeks ago in the bracken on Shooter's Hill. Otto must have found it and put it in his pack.'

Martha smiled. 'Perhaps the new fence has brought us luck. We have all our things back, Otto is not going to steal again and I shall be able to buy cheap wool.'

'Huh!' said Thomas.

Historical Notes
for The Pedlar

In medieval England many farm workers had strips of land to cultivate and were allowed grazing rights on common land. After the Black Death in the 14th century when the wool trade increased, landowners enclosed more land. In Tudor times, with a bigger population, landowners started to raise large flocks to provide wool and meat. But they needed fences to secure their flocks, so even more land and woods were fenced and access denied to the villagers. Inside the fences, the sheep ate all the villagers' crops and the woods were cut down to sow more grass.

Although anti-enclosure Acts were passed by Henry the Seventh, Henry the Eighth and Elizabeth the First, these had little effect and poor people became even poorer and sometimes homeless. When Henry the Eighth became king, poor people could still get help from the monasteries but he later closed the monasteries and many poor people became vagrants, begging and robbing out of desperation. Vagrants were given harsh punishments.

There is a catchpole in this story. A catchpole was like a village constable and could arrest people and take them to the nearest lock-up. The wrongdoer was then tried by a magistrate who was a local rich man. The magistrate decided whether the criminal deserved prison, or another punishment, or freedom. Sometimes magistrates were lenient but sometimes they were cruel and gave harsh punishments.

Glossary

Jerkin – A waistcoat.

Spinning wheel – Used to spin fleece into strands for weaving. Most cottages had such a wheel.

Pedlar – Travelling man who went from house to house selling goods from a pack.

Bracken – A wild fern growing on hillsides.

Catchpole – The village constable.

Magistrate – A man who laid down the law and gave out sentences and punishments.

BONES AT THE FAIR

Sir Paul stood in the narrow street and looked up at the front of his house. Good timber beams. Painted plaster walls. Windows with glass. Strong front door. Bedrooms jutting out over the downstairs rooms. It was a fine house.

'Hannah!' he shouted. A young servant in a white apron came out of the house and <u>curtsied</u>. 'Hannah, it is Statutes Day. There will be all sorts of strangers about, so see that the door is always shut. And make sure that Bones does not get out.'

Bones was the family dog. He didn't like being kept inside the house. Best of all he liked running down the market street and being a nuisance to the stall-holders.

Hannah followed Sir Paul into the house, shutting the door carefully after them. Outside, in the street, people were gathering. There were townsfolk, villagers from nearby, farmers and their families, children and old people. Mixed in with them were the fair's people – jugglers, card tricksters, acrobats, stilt walkers, street singers, men selling fruit, cooked food and drinks. They all wore colourful clothes.

In the house, Bones the dog was behind the door. He sniffed. He could smell food outside in the street. He could smell other dogs too and he could smell rats in the drain which ran down the middle of the street.

Hannah came down the dark hallway to check that the door was still closed. When she reached the door she heard a <u>lute</u> playing out in the street and someone singing. She knew the tune. It was a country song and the words made her think of her home. She felt sad when she heard it. She only had one day's holiday each year so she hardly ever went home.

The song ended but Hannah wanted to see the singer so she opened the door.

WHIZZ!

Bones the dog shot between her legs, out of the door, down the steps and into the crowd.

Hannah called him back but he had gone. Sir Paul would be very angry. She took off her apron and ran after Bones.

There was a baker's stall in the <u>cobbled</u> street. It had been full of bread, cakes, meat pies and sweet things. But now the stall was lying on its side and the cakes and pies were

strewn in the road. Some of them had already been grabbed by some passing boys.

The baker was red-faced and angry. 'I'll kill that dog!' he yelled. 'It rushed past and hit the table leg.'

'It must have been Bones,' thought Hannah but she didn't stop. She ran on down the hill. At the bottom, there was a juggler in <u>jester's</u> clothes sitting on the cobbles. 'My juggling balls!' he moaned. 'I dropped them all when that dog flew past and ran under my feet. Now they have all rolled away.'

Bones was sitting nearby. In his mouth was a large blue and white ball. The ball was made of wool which was wound round a wooden ball. One of the juggler's lost balls. 'Bones!' shouted Hannah. 'Drop it!'

Bones dropped the ball on the ground and looked up at Hannah. She bent down to pick it up, but Bones was too quick. He snatched the ball away and ran towards the river. On his way he crashed into a clothes stall and upturned it.

Hannah looked up at the sky. Storm clouds were gathering and it was beginning to rain. She sighed and ran after Bones.

Bones was covered in splashes of mud and the juggler's ball was just a ragged lump in his mouth. He stopped to sniff at the drain in the middle of the street. It was full of all sorts of smelly rubbish floating down to the river. Bones followed the smells.

It was raining really hard when Bones reached the edge of the river. Everything was slippery. Hannah shouted at him again. Bones stopped and looked back, but then he lost his footing. His front feet slithered down the slimy river bank and he was in the water.

Hannah was very frightened. If she went back without the dog there would be real trouble. She might even lose her job. She slithered down the river bank, lifted her skirts and waded into the water after Bones.

When she reached him, Bones jumped up at her, spraying her with filthy water. Hannah shut her eyes and felt the mud and water wash all over her. Then she slipped and suddenly she was in fast-moving, deep water up to her neck.

Bones could swim but Hannah could not.

A boatman saved her. He had heard Bones barking. He hauled her into his boat and

rowed her to the bank. Bones followed. They both collapsed in a heap beside the filthy drain while the boatman tied up his boat.

But Hannah wasn't safe for long. When the boatman came back he shouted, 'Quick, move to higher ground, the water is rising.'

The water was getting deeper and deeper.

There was water everywhere. Higher up the street, by the shops, people were shouting 'Flood!'

Some men ran down the hill to the river bank. They began to shovel earth against it. Everybody was soaking wet. Water was flowing down the street, splashing against the walls.

Bones rubbed his head against Hannah's legs. She dragged him through the flood and away. At last they reached their house.

Sir Paul was at the door, looking at the water rushing past his steps.

'Don't bring that dog in here,' he called. 'He's filthy and he smells – and you are dripping water, too. Where have you been with him, you stupid girl?'

Hannah started to tell him, but a man ran past. He was shouting, 'They've made the bank higher. The water's going down.'

'Any shops flooded?' asked Sir Paul.

'Some,' said the man, stopping to catch his breath. 'But my master was lucky. His clothes shop was saved. Saved by a dog!'

'A dog? How was that?' asked Sir Paul.

The man laughed. 'A dog knocked over our stall and the clothes fell into the street. So my master had us all outside picking them up. We had just finished when the rain started. We put the shutters up and rammed old rags under the door. So the shop has stayed dry.'

Then he noticed Hannah and Bones. The man pointed at Bones. 'That's him,' he shouted. 'That's the dog that saved the shop! He deserves a reward.'

Bones bounded up the steps and into the house, leaving mud and filth everywhere.

'Reward?' said Sir Paul, as he and Hannah followed.

'I'll give him a reward. Drat the dog! His reward will be no supper and a cold bath in the yard.'

Outside the rain had stopped. The flood drained away. Down the street a trumpet sounded, music began to play and the sun came out. The fair and procession were starting. Everything was going to be all right.

Historical Notes
for Bones at the Fair

Statutes Day came once a year and was special. Towns and villages were given permission to close shops for the day, if they chose. Normal work stopped. Visiting music makers, dancers, clowns and other entertainers arrived. The street was cleared, stalls were set up to sell sweets and food and drink. Everybody enjoyed themselves.

Men who worked on farms often changed their jobs on Statutes Day. Groups of them stood around in certain spots and farmers who needed help chose men from the groups to work for them for a year.

Shops with openings on to the street served as usual. Some of them put stalls out in front. The street and house fronts were swept clean.

Often the main town drain ran down the middle of the road. This took away waste water, sewage, and anything else thrown into it, no matter how smelly or nasty. The drain flowed into a stream or river, but sometimes, in heavy rain, rivers and drains overflowed and everything ran across the road and into the houses and shops.

Glossary

Curtsey – Girls and ladies curtsey by bending their knees and holding out the edge of their skirts.

Juggler – Man who amuses people by throwing up and catching a number of balls or other objects.

Trickster – Someone who tricks people into parting with their money.

Lute – Musical instrument rather like a guitar.

Cobbles – Round hard stones laid down to make a path or street.

Jester – A jester was often employed by royalty or noblemen to entertain them. They wore distinctive and colourful clothes, called Motley'.

THE NAMESAKE

The city of London was crowded. The streets were busy, the River Thames was even busier. Large ships were tied up at the quays, unloading goods from lands across the seas. There were big pots of spices, baskets of rare fruits and bales of fine cloth. A ship from Spain had a cargo of wonderful swords, spears and shiny armour.

There were small ferry boats, too, criss-crossing the river, carrying people from one side to the other.

London Bridge was busy with people hurrying past and children looking down at the boats. A sedan chair came by, carried by four large men. A little side curtain was open and a lady was leaning out. She was shouting at the men to hurry. 'I'm going to the theatre,' she yelled. 'You must get me there before the Queen arrives. She goes to see the play today.'

In a house not far away lived a young woman called Jane. Her husband, Walter, had sailed his ship to France. He had gone to buy wine to sell in their wine-shop.

Walter had been gone for some time and Jane was getting worried. Their baby was due and Jane should be at her sister's for the birth. But her sister Anne lived on the other side of the river and Walter had left no money to pay the ferryman to take Jane across.

Jane sighed and looked out of the window. The street was noisy and crowded, and it was getting dark. In the gloom, she saw two men standing outside her house. Quickly, Jane drew back from the window, her heart beating fast.

One of the men was the landlord's son. He was a harsh man and she knew why he was there. He had come for the rent and he would do anything to get it from her.

But what could she do? Her husband was away and she had no money to give him.

She had a bag with clothes in, ready to take to her sister's. Jane picked it up, crammed a hat over her eyes and dashed out of the front door.

'That's her!' she heard a man shout. Somebody was running after her.

Jane ran as fast as she could but she began to feel faint. She forced herself to keep going but then, suddenly, everything went black and she collapsed.

When she opened her eyes she saw a face that she knew. It was Sir John Copes, a rich gentleman. She had worked for his family before her marriage. 'Why, Jane,' Sir John said. 'I was coming to see you. My wife wondered how you were. Can you stand up?'

Jane stood up and rubbed her eyes. 'Oh Sir John,' she said. 'Thank God you came. Those men were chasing me.'

Sir John smiled. 'They've gone, Jane. Now get into my carriage and I will take you home.'

Jane told him that her sister was waiting for her and that her husband was away at sea and had left no money.

'Don't worry,' said Sir John. 'We'll go down to the river and get a ferry to take you across to your sister's house.'

Half an hour later Jane was sitting in a small ferry. The ferryman had been paid and she was on her way across the river.

* * *

On the other bank stood a new playhouse. A play was to be performed that day, and Queen Elizabeth was coming to see it. Up on the straw roof some men were repairing a hole made by a flock of starlings. They had finished but they were hoping to stay on and see the Queen.

Down on the stage the actors were standing around. They were very worried. One of their company was ill. The chief actor, Adam, was shouting at all the others. 'We cannot do the play without him. And the Queen is coming to the performance. What can we do?' He looked up to the sky and shouted, 'Please God, send me an actor!'

One of the men on the roof was Ben. His mother was Jane's sister, Anne. Ben was very interested in what was happening on

the stage. He leaned forward to see and caught his foot in a bundle of straw. He fell through the roof and landed with a crash on the stage just in front of Adam.

'A miracle!' said Adam. 'I asked for an actor and one drops at my feet! Get up, lad. It's worth a silver crown if you take the part.'

Ben pulled straw out of his hair. 'Well, I would like a crown,' he said. 'But I have never acted. What do I have to do?'

'Never mind that,' said Adam. 'You'll find out soon enough.' He turned to the others. 'Here you lot, take him to the dressing room and put him in costume. Teach him some of the lines while you dress him. And hurry up, the Queen will be here soon.'

Ten minutes later Ben came back. He was wearing a woman's dress and apron. His face was red. 'You never said it was a woman's part,' he said.

Adam grinned. 'All women's parts are played by boys. No women go on stage. Now, are you ready?'

* * *

Out on the river Jane's ferry was jammed in between some boats. 'Hurry up,' she said to the ferryman. 'My baby is on the way.'

'Oh no!' said the ferryman. 'The Queen is about to appear and you having a ...' Then he stopped talking because everyone on the river started cheering. They had seen the royal <u>barge</u>.

The barge was crowded with ladies and gentlemen, all dressed in rich clothes. The men wore hats with feathers and had swords by their sides. The women had long jewelled dresses and their faces were white with powder.

Seated on a padded chair in the barge was a slim lady in white. Diamonds sparkled on her dress and her sash. More were in her hair. It was Queen Elizabeth.

But Jane didn't notice. She was moaning and crying. She could feel her baby coming.

As the royal barge was being rowed past the ferry, the Queen saw Jane. She held up her hand. 'Stop the barge,' she said. 'That girl in the ferry is in trouble.' She called to two young noblemen. 'You two, fetch the girl here and we'll take her to the shore.'

The two young men did as they were told but as Jane was helped on to the barge she started screaming. 'My baby!' she cried. 'My baby is coming.'

The two men started to take her back to the ferry but the Queen stopped them. She beckoned to the women who stood around her. 'Don't just stand there. Help the lady, some of you popinjay women. Help the poor child.'

In just a few minutes Jane's baby was safely born. It was a lovely girl. The Queen was smiling. 'Give the mother a drink,' she said. 'And pass the baby to me to hold. I shall never have a child of my own.' She held the baby for a while and then she said, 'Listen, all of you. I want this child to be called Elizabeth.' She turned to Jane. 'And I want you to tell your daughter that the Queen of England was the first person to hold her.'

'God save the Queen!' everybody shouted as the barge rowed for the shore. Jane and the baby were lifted off and put in a coach. The Queen watched them go. 'Now for the play,' she said.

* * *

Jane was soon in the care of her sister, wrapped warmly and sitting by the fire. Her sister Anne kept on saying, 'I can't believe it. The Queen held the baby and the baby's to be called after her.'

Jane smiled. 'Yes,' she said, looking down at little Elizabeth. 'She's the Queen's namesake.'

Then the door opened and Walter, Jane's husband, came in. There were hugs and kisses and the story of Jane's adventure was told again and again. Food and drink were put out.

'What a wonderful day,' said Walter. 'And my trip was good as well.'

In the middle of it all, the door opened again and in walked a very strange creature. His face was covered with powder and coloured marks. His eyes were shaded by black eyelashes. And worst of all he was wearing a woman's dress.

Anne jumped up. 'It's my boy! It's Ben! Ben, what are you doing? Why are you dressed like that? Have you gone mad?'

'No,' Ben said. 'Not mad. I've been on the stage, acting in front of the Queen. And what's more, I am a roof worker no longer. Master Adam at the playhouse has said I can be an actor. He wants me to go round the country with his players. We shall act the plays in towns and at rich houses. *And* he will pay me much more than I get now. Isn't that wonderful news? I bet nothing as exciting has happened to any of you today.'

And he wondered why everybody started laughing.

Historical Notes
for The Namesake

In the sixteenth century big cities did not have as many people living in them as we have today. There were only thousands where we now have millions. Most poor people lived in houses owned by the rich. They paid rents, but if they did not pay on time the landlord would send men round to turn them out of their homes.

In London, the River Thames was like a main road. There were no cars or taxis, of course, in those days, but people got about by riding on boats up and down and across the river. Boats that charged passengers were called ferries and all of them had to be rowed with oars.

At the time of this story Queen Elizabeth the First was on the throne. She was fond of plays and new theatres were being built, especially on the South bank of the river. They were built in the shape of a horse-shoe, were open air except for rows of seats on balconies round the stage. A lot of people with little money went inside and stood round the stage. They were known as groundlings. William Shakespeare was a famous playwright at the time.

Glossary

Quay – A landing place on the river bank for goods and passengers.

Spices – In Queen Elizabeth the First's time, food often went bad. The smell and taste of spices made it edible. Most spices were brought to England from Asia and Africa. Cargoes of spices made a lot of money.

Sedan chair – A covered chair for one person to sit in while strong men carried the chair on poles.

Barge – Large flat-bottomed boat.

Popinjay – A silly person, often foolishly dressed, who behaved stupidly.